EDDIE
and TEDDY

For James and Frank

Copyright © 1990 by Gus Clarke
First published in Great Britain by Andersen Press, Ltd. 1990
All rights reserved. No part of this book may be reproduced or utilized in any
form or by any means, electronic or mechanical, including photocopying,
recording or by any information storage and retrieval system, without per-
mission in writing from the Publisher. Inquiries should be addressed to
Lothrop, Lee & Shepard Books, a division of William Morrow & Company, Inc.,
1350 Avenue of the Americas, New York, NY 10019. First U.S. Edition, 1991.
First Mulberry Edition, 1992. Printed in the U.S.A.

10 9 8 7 6 5 4 3 2 1

Library of Congress Cataloging in Publication Data
Clarke, Gus. Eddie and Teddy / Gus Clarke.
p.   cm. Summary: Having been inseparable from his teddy bear for years,
Eddie has to leave Teddy behind when he starts school. ISBN 0-688-11700-7.
[1. Teddy bears—Fiction.   2. Schools—Fiction]   I. Title.   PZ7.C5534Ed 1991
[E]—dc20   90-5795 CIP

EDDIE
and TEDDY

Gus Clarke

Mulberry Books, New York

Eddie and Teddy were the very best of friends.

Wherever they went...

...and whatever they did,

they went, and they did it, together.

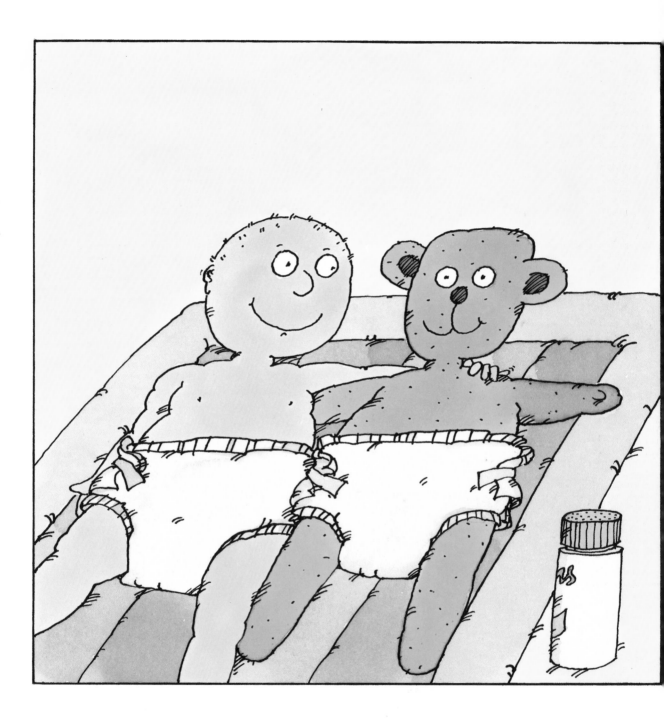

They'd been together for years and years. Eddie just couldn't remember a time when Teddy hadn't been there. They'd shared every moment.

When Eddie had gone to see Santa Claus...

...Teddy had gone as well.

And when Eddie fell off the kitchen table and banged his head...

. . . Teddy fell too.

So, one day, when Eddie went to Big School and Mom said Teddy should stay at home, Eddie was very upset.

So was Teddy.

But Eddie had lots of new things to do and people to meet.
He soon cheered up.

Teddy didn't.

Mom tried everything: a story with a cuddle,

a walk in the park to feed the ducks,

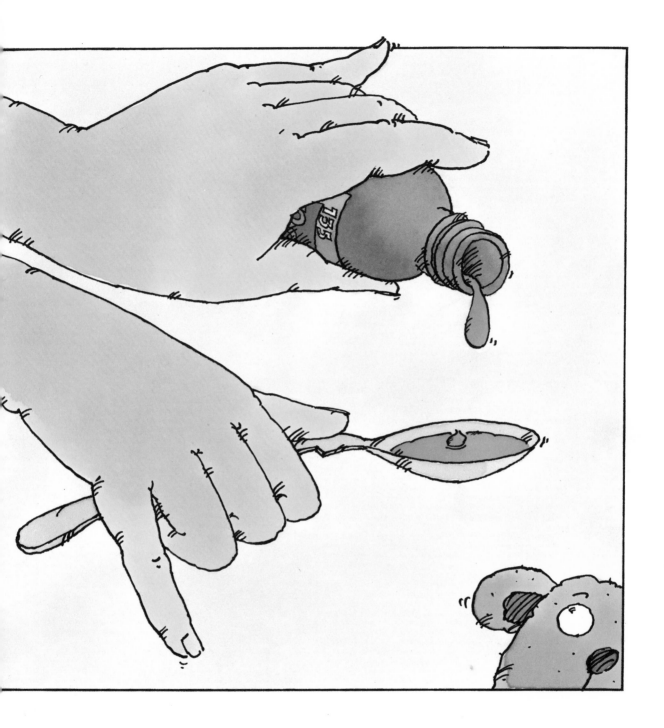

even some of the very special Pink Medicine,

but it didn't help.

In the end, Mom could stand it no more and sent him upstairs.

She was very glad when it was time to pick up Eddie
from school.

So was Teddy.

Eddie told him all about his day,

and Mom told Eddie all about hers. Eddie felt very sorry for Teddy.

That night, Mom had a word with Eddie's teacher,

and the next day, when she took Eddie to school, Teddy went too.

He was as good as gold,

and has been ever since, from that day . . .

...to this.